A [illegible]dge Between Worlds

Adapted by ELIZABETH LENHARD

This book was first published in the USA in 2004 by Volo/Hyperion Books for Children
First published in Great Britain in 2006 by HarperCollins *Children's Books*, a division of HarperCollins Publishers Ltd.

ISBN 13: 978-0-00-720945-3
ISBN 0-00-720945-2

1 3 5 7 9 10 8 6 4 2

The HarperCollins website is:
www.harpercollinschildrensbooks.co.uk

Visit www.clubwitch.co.uk

Printed and bound in Italy

IN A FLASH, THE ENTIRE PRISON OF MERIDIAN DISAPPEARS.
ELYON ERASES THIS. . . . FOR THE WOMAN WHOM, DEEP IN HER HEART, SHE STILL CONSIDERS TO BE HER MOTHER. . . .
. . . AND FOR THE CITIZENS SHE IS BEGINNING TO THINK OF AS . . .
. . . HER OWN PEOPLE.

ONE INSTANT. . .
OH!
ONE GLANCE . . .
ELYON?
ONE WORD. . .
MUM?
SOMETIMES, IT TAKES VERY LITTLE TO CHANGE PEOPLE'S DESTINY.
IT'S HER! ELYON! THE LIGHT OF MERIDIAN!
OR TO DIVIDE A PEOPLE.
DID YOU SEE THAT? SHE DESTROYED THE PRISON.
LONG LIVE THE LIGHT OF MERIDIAN!
SHE'S COME FOR US. FOR US!

ELYON!
SHE'S TOO FAR AWAY, CORNELIA! LET'S GO. IT'LL BE EASIER TO DISAPPEAR IN THE MIDDLE OF THIS CROWD.
THESE REBELS WILL TAKE US TO SAFETY, ELEANOR. LET'S GO.
I'M COMING, THOMAS. DID YOU HEAR HER?
DID YOU HEAR WHAT SHE CALLED ME?
MUM!

MERIDIAN,
INSIDE PHOBOS'S CASTLE . . .
I HAVE FAILED, MY LORD. I DID NOT SUCCEED IN DESTROYING THE TWO TRAITORS.
I KNOW, CEDRIC. I KNOW ALL ABOUT IT.
PLEASE EXPLAIN TO ME HOW ELYON WAS ABLE TO MAKE THE PRISON JUST DISAPPEAR.
I REALISE HER POWER IS IMMENSE. THAT IS WHY I WANT IT FOR MYSELF!
AND WHY IT IS TIME TO OFFICIALLY ANNOUNCE HER CORONATION.
HEATHERFIELD,
IN ELYON'S BASEMENT. . .
THINGS ARE DEFINITELY CHANGING IN MERIDIAN.
SO I WASN'T WRONG ABOUT ELYON. SHE UNDERSTANDS WHAT'S GOING ON. SHE NEEDS US.
WHAT ARE YOU DOING, CORNELIA?
I'M MAKING A WALL TO HIDE THE PORTAL. WE MIGHT NEED TO USE IT AGAIN.
CRAAAMM
WITHOUT THE MAP OF THE PORTALS, IT'S THE ONLY ONE THAT WE KNOW ABOUT, AND. . .
SHHHH! SOMEONE'S COMING. WE'D BETTER CHANGE BACK, QUICK!

THIS WAY, MCTIENNAN! I KNOW I SAW A LIGHT COMING FROM THE BASEMENT.
THAT'S STRANGE. THE ELECTRICITY'S OUT.
HI! WHAT BRINGS YOU FOLKS HERE?
WE THOUGHT YOU MIGHT BE HERE.
BUT WE COULD ASK YOU THE SAME QUESTION.
LATER ON, IN FRONT OF CORNELIA'S HOUSE . . .
THANKS FOR GOING WITH ME, WILL. THANKS FOR EVERYTHING!
NO PROBLEM! THE IMPORTANT THING IS THAT WE SHOOK OFF THOSE AGENTS.
DO YOU THINK THEY BOUGHT THE STORY ABOUT HAVING A GET-TOGETHER IN MEMORY OF ELYON AT HER HOUSE?
I DOUBT IT. BUT I COULDN'T COME UP WITH ANYTHING BETTER. . .

". . . AND AGENT MEDINA REALLY SHOWED US HOW TOUGH SHE WAS."
LET'S JUST GO! WE HAVE NO REASON TO KEEP THE GIRLS ANY LONGER.
I'M TELLING YOU, THERE WAS A GIANT IN THE BACK OF THIS VAN. A REAL MONSTER AND . . .

YEAH, YOU'RE RIGHT! THAT'S ONE GIANT. . . DOG!
WOOF
WOOF

HELLO, THERE. DID YOU FOLLOW ME ALL THE WAY HERE?
AAAAH-CHOOO!
YEAH, AND WE HAD TO RENT A CAR TO DO IT.
THAT WAS VERY NICE OF YOU, BUT THERE WAS NO NEED. I KNOW HOW TO CHANGE GEARS NOW.
LET'S GO! SNIFF! I'M ALLERGIC TO WISE GUYS. . . . AND DOG FUR.
MAYBE VATHEK WAS ALLERGIC TO HIM, TOO. THAT COULD BE WHY HE WAS SNEEZING SO MUCH.
BY THE WAY, THIS MUST BE HIS! I FOUND IT IN THE VAN!
A TOKEN. WHY DO YOU THINK IT'S VATHEK'S?
I DON'T KNOW. IT'S JUST A FUNNY FEELING! I CAN SENSE SOME SORT OF VIBRATION.
TAKING THE DOG WAS A GREAT IDEA.
"WHEN WE GOT BACK TO THE SHOP, WE FOUND MATT'S REAL GRANDFATHER, TAKING A NAP. . . ."
I NEEDED AN EXCUSE TO EXPLAIN MR. OLSEN'S ASTRAL DROP TO MATT!

"INSTINCTIVELY, THE ASTRAL DROP WENT BACK INTO HIS TWIN'S BODY. . . .
". . . WHICH GAVE HIM THE MEMORY OF EVERYTHING THAT HAD HAPPENED. . . ."
I HAD THE STRANGEST DREAM! YOU WERE THERE, WILL. AND THERE WAS THIS BIG, BLUE GIANT DRESSED AS A WOMAN. . . .
IS THAT WHEN YOU FOUND MATT'S NOTE?
YUP! AN OFFICIAL INVITATION TO THE LODELDAY. THE COOLEST PLACE IN THE WHOLE CITY!
XWILL
WILL! DID IT OCCUR TO YOU THAT FOR THE FIRST TIME SINCE THIS WHOLE THING STARTED, WE'RE GETTING ALONG PERFECTLY?
IT DID! BUT THEN, WE'RE NOT REALLY SO DIFFERENT.
YOU KNOW WHAT I THINK? I THINK THAT FROM NOW ON, THINGS ARE GOING TO JUST KEEP GETTING BETTER!
XWILL
SIMULTECH, AN INDUSTRIAL COMPANY ON THE OUTSKIRTS OF HEATHERFIELD . . .
THIS COMPANY CAN'T AFFORD TO LOSE A GREAT WORKER LIKE YOU, SUSAN.
YOU WON'T REALLY BE LOSING ME. I'M JUST ASKING FOR A TRANSFER.
SIMULTECH INDUSTRIES

LEVIN BISHOP
HUMAN RESOURCES DIRECTOR
WILL DOESN'T LIKE HEATHERFIELD. OUR RELATIONSHIP IS DETERIORATING, AND I DON'T WANT TO LOSE HER.
HAVE YOU THOUGHT EVEN A LITTLE ABOUT YOURSELF? ABOUT YOUR HAPPINESS? YOU MENTIONED A TEACHER. . . .
DEAN WILL HAVE TO UNDERSTAND. MY LITTLE GIRL IS MY WHOLE FAMILY.
IF IT IS WHAT YOU WANT. BUT I NEED TO TALK THIS OVER WITH THE BOARD.
IF YOUR REQUEST IS GRANTED, YOU'LL HAVE A NEW POSITION IN ANOTHER CITY BY SUMMER-TIME.
THANKS, LEVIN. THAT WAY WILL CAN FINISH UP HER SCHOOL YEAR WITHOUT ANY MORE TRAUMA.
NOW, ALL I HAVE TO DO IS FIND A WAY TO TELL HER.
"YESSS! FROM NOW ON, THINGS ARE GOING TO GET A LOT BETTER. . . ."
WILL
TO BE CONTINUED . . .

ELYON'S HOUSE, ON THE OUTSKIRTS OF HEATHERFIELD . . .
FROUUSH

THE ELECTRICITY'S OUT. MAYBE WE'D BETTER POSTPONE THE INSPECTION.

I DON'T THINK SO. IT'S NOT EVERY DAY AN ENTIRE FAMILY DISAPPEARS INTO THIN AIR!

WHAT DO WE HAVE HERE?

CRAAACK
ELYON

DRAWINGS BY ELYON BROWN, FROM WHEN SHE WAS SIX UNTIL RIGHT BEFORE HER DISAPPEARANCE. INTERESTING!
DADDY
MUMMY
ELYON

HMMM. THERE'S A RECURRING IMAGE. IT LOOKS LIKE A MAGICAL CITY.

LOOK! THIS ONE IS COMPLETE. THE CITY, AGAIN. AND ABOVE IT. . .

. . . A GIRL WEARING A CROWN. FLYING AROUND AND SHINING LIKE THE SUN.

LOOKS LIKE DROPS OF WATER FELL RIGHT ON HER FACE. THE COLOURS ARE ALL SMEARED. TOO BAD.

OH, ELYON! WHERE ARE YOU? WHAT HAPPENED TO YOU?
KNOCK KNOCK
MAY I COME IN?

UM . . . AGENT LAIR? HEADQUARTERS TOLD YOU WE WERE COMING, RIGHT?
YES. I'M A DETECTIVE, TOO, BUT NOT LIKE YOU FOLKS FROM INTERPOL.
NICE TO MEET YOU. I'M MARIA MEDINA, THE PSYCHOLOGIST – FROM THE MISSING PERSONS DIVISION.
BUT ALL THIS HAPPENED MONTHS AGO. WHY THE SUDDEN INTEREST?
THE CASE WAS SUBMITTED TO US JUST RECENTLY. BUT WE'VE ALREADY NOTICED SOME DISCREPANCIES.
FOR INSTANCE?
FOR INSTANCE, THE FACT THAT THE BROWN FAMILY DOESN'T EVEN EXIST!
THIS IS MY COLLEAGUE, JOEL MCTIERNAN. HE DOESN'T TALK MUCH. . . . BUT WHEN HE DOES, HE TELLS IT LIKE IT IS.
WHAT ARE YOU TALKING ABOUT? THEY DON'T EXIST? THE HEATHERFIELD CITY HALL HAS DOCUMENTS THAT. . .
. . . THAT ARE FALSE! WE HAD THEM EXAMINED BY OUR EXPERTS. WE'RE WELL INFORMED.
BY THE WAY . . . ONE OF THESE GIRLS IS YOUR DAUGHTER, CORRECT?

"YES, BUT IT LOOKS LIKE YOU'RE NOT AS WELL INFORMED AS YOU THOUGHT. THE GIRL YOU'RE POINTING TO IS . . ."
WILL! WIIILL!
WHOOSH
SHUT THE DOOR! IT'S GETTING CRAZY IN HERE.
CIP CIP CIP CIP CIP
SQUAWK
MEOW
MEOW
WOOF
YAP YAP YAP
SLAM
WHEW! HI, MATT. WHAT A DAY. . .
WHAT?
HUH?

THAT'S INCREDIBLE! A SECOND AGO THEY WERE GOING CRAZY! BUT THE MUMENT THEY HEARD YOUR VOICE. . .
UM . . . MUST BE A COINCIDENCE.
LOOK AT PEPE. HE'S EATING NOW. HE HADN'T TOUCHED HIS FOOD ALL DAY.
PEPE FOOD! FOOD! SQUAWK!
MATT DOESN'T KNOW THAT ANIMALS ARE . . . WHAT'S THE WORD? EMPATHETIC! THEY REACT TO MY MOOD.
HAVE I EVER THANKED YOU FOR WHAT YOU'VE DONE FOR THE SHOP?
AND RIGHT NOW, I'M IN A REALLY GREAT MOOD!
TOYS
DON'T MENTION IT. YOU KNOW I LIKE HELPING OUT YOUR GRANDFATHER.
I KNOW, BUT YOU GAVE UP YOUR VACATION! AND FOR WHAT?
JUST TO HANG AROUND THESE ANIM –
AROUND YOU! SQUAWK! AROUND YOU!
?

I COULD SWEAR THAT PEPE JUST . . .
. . . JUST STARTED RAMBLING! JUST AN OLD, BALDING PARROT, SQUAWKING AWAY.
FORGET EMPATHETIC. THESE ANIMALS KNOW WHAT I'M THINKING!
THINKING! SQUAWK! THINKING!
NOW THAT'S A PARTY! DID YOU SEE WHO LIVENED UP NEW YEAR'S EVE AT THE LODELDAY?
I'VE HEARD ABOUT THAT PLACE! IT'S HEATHERFIELD'S MOST EXPENSIVE RESTAURANT.
JACKIE GILLIGAN. YOU MET HER. REMEMBER?
GRUNT! WHO COULD FORGET A FAKE LIKE HER?
FAKE! FA – GNFFF!
GULP! I'LL HAVE TO BE A BIT MORE CAREFUL ABOUT WHAT I THINK.
I TOLD YOU ALL ABOUT HER. . . . I USED TO HAVE A CRUSH ON HER. I EVEN WANTED TO INVITE HER TO THE LODELDAY!
REMAIN CALM, WILL! STAY CALM!
SHE REALLY THREW ME! NOT BECAUSE SHE WAS A KNOCKOUT OR OLDER THAN ME OR ANYTHING LIKE THAT. I THINK IT'S BECAUSE SHE ALWAYS KNEW HOW TO SURPRISE ME!
GRRRR